Tickets!

Written by Alice Hemming

Illustrated by Mike Byrne

Collins

Trish packs a travel bag for her trip.

The ticket man needs to stamp
her ticket.

4

Trish checks the pockets of
her sundress.

7

Trish checks her panda lunchbox.

It is a crisp sandwich for lunch.

Crunch!

Did she stash it with her flip flops? No!

The man offers to sell Trish a ticket.

Trish hunts for her credit card in her handbag.

13

Ticket

After reading

Letters and Sounds: Phase 4

Word count: 100

Focus on adjacent consonants with short vowel phonemes, e.g. l/o/st

Common exception words: the, she, my, here, you, some, of, have, I, to, no

Curriculum links (EYFS): Understanding the World: People and communities

Curriculum links (National Curriculum, Year 1): PSHE

Early learning goals: Reading: use phonic knowledge to decode regular words and read them aloud accurately; demonstrate understanding when talking with others about what they have read

National Curriculum learning objectives: Reading/word reading: apply phonic knowledge and skills as the route to decode words; read accurately by blending sounds in unfamiliar words containing GPCs that have been taught; read other words of more than one syllable that contain taught GPCs; read aloud accurately books that are consistent with their developing phonic knowledge; re-read books to build up their fluency and confidence in word reading; Reading/comprehension: link what they have read or hear read to their own experiences; discuss word meanings; discuss the significance of the title and events

Developing fluency

- Your child may enjoy listening to you read the whole book.
- Model using expression and voices to read the speech bubbles.

Phonic practice

- Ask your child:
  - Can you think of any words that rhyme with **stamp**? (e.g. *damp, lamp, ramp, camp*)
  - Can you think of any words that rhyme with **stuck**? (e.g. *luck, duck, truck*)

Extending vocabulary

- Trish "crunches" her sandwich. What other words can we use to describe eating? (e.g. *munch, chew, gulp, swallow, chomp*)
- Trish finds a damp dishcloth in her pocket. How can you describe the sound of water dripping? (e.g. *drip drop, splash, splish, plop, trickle, splatter*)